D1200632

OMA FINDS A
MIRACLE

Story by

Patrick "Packy" Mader

Illustrated by

Andrew Holmquist

Beaver's Pond Press, Inc.

ISBN-13: 978-1-59298-181-6
ISBN-10: 1-59298-181-X

Library of Congress Catalog Number: 2007921303

Printed in the United States of America

First Printing: February 2007

11 10 09 08 07   5 4 3 2 1

Thanks to Stan, Greg, and George Mader for their support and encouragement
Edited by Catherine Friend
Project management and advice provided by Milt Adams, Kellie Hultgren, and Judith Palmateer, Beaver's Pond Press
Design, layout, and typesetting by Mori Studio, Inc.

Beaver's Pond Press, Inc.

7104 Ohms Lane, Suite 216
Edina, MN 55439
(952) 829-8818
www.BeaversPondPress.com

To order, visit www.BookHouseFulfillment.com
or call 1-800-901-3480. Reseller discounts available.

For more information visit www.patrickmader.com

DEDICATIONS

To Grandma Marcy Olson
a city girl who gave her family a taste of country life
—and—
Karen, Karl, and Ellen
miracles in my own life
P.M.

To Sue, Chris, and Matt
my greatest supporters
A.H.

One wintry day Oma and her grandchildren were gathered in the kitchen at Oma and Opa's farm in Minnesota. Oma is a German word for grandma. Opa is a German word for grandpa.

As the snow swirled outside, the grandchildren asked Oma to tell them a story.

Oma mixed the cookie dough, watched the blowing snow out the kitchen window, and she remembered…

"I will tell you a story that happened thirty years ago. It's about the time I found a miracle," said Oma.

One late November day, when Oma was younger and had to care for seven children, the cows grazed on cornstalks in the far field by the woods. It began to snow, but the cows kept grazing until the middle of the afternoon.

As the cows came home, Oma saw that the almost-all-white cow trailed far behind the others and kept looking back toward the field. Oma's seven children, who always chose perfect names for the animals, had named this cow Presto.

When the children came home from school, they had a snack and did their chores as usual. Then the children had lots of fun sledding and tobogganing in the fresh snow.

As Oma watched her children play, she wondered about the slow return of Presto. Since Opa was away from the farm that day building a house, Oma decided to go to the barn to check on the cow. As Oma patted Presto, she thought the cow had sad eyes and looked thinner than she had that morning. Suddenly Oma knew what had happened.

Oma called the children together and told them there might be a newborn calf in the far field by the woods. The three oldest children hurried through the deepening snow to search for a calf. They talked about choosing a perfect name for it.

It was a long walk, though, and in the whirling snow they saw only white. The three children looked until the day darkened and then trudged home.

It stopped snowing that night, but the children worried about the newborn calf outside, alone, in the snow and cold. Oma and Opa worried too. They said it would be a miracle for a calf to live through such a night.

After Opa milked the cows in the morning, he left to work on the inside of the house he was building, and the children left, sadly, to go to school. They were still worried about the newborn calf.

Oma went to the barn to check on the cows and looked into the sad eyes of Presto. Then Oma had an idea.

The new snow was deep and the cornstalks were hidden, but maybe Presto still could find her newborn calf. Oma let Presto out of the barn and followed her. They plowed a deep and thin trail to the far field near the woods. It took a long time.

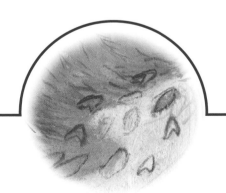

Then the almost-all-white cow stopped, stretched her neck down, and gave the snow a sniff and a lick. But it wasn't snow…it was an all-white newborn calf!

No wonder the three children had been unable to find it in the whirling white snow. The calf was cold and stiff, but it was alive.

"I have found a miracle," thought Oma as she hurried home.

"But how will I ever get this newborn calf to the warm barn? The snow is too deep and the trail is too narrow for a tractor or the old, rusty pick-up truck."

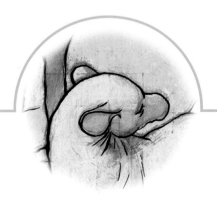

When Oma finally got back to the farmyard, she looked around for a way to help bring the all-white calf back to the barn.

And then she saw the children's toboggan.

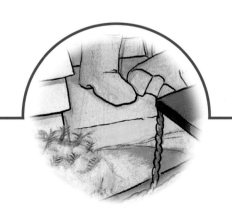

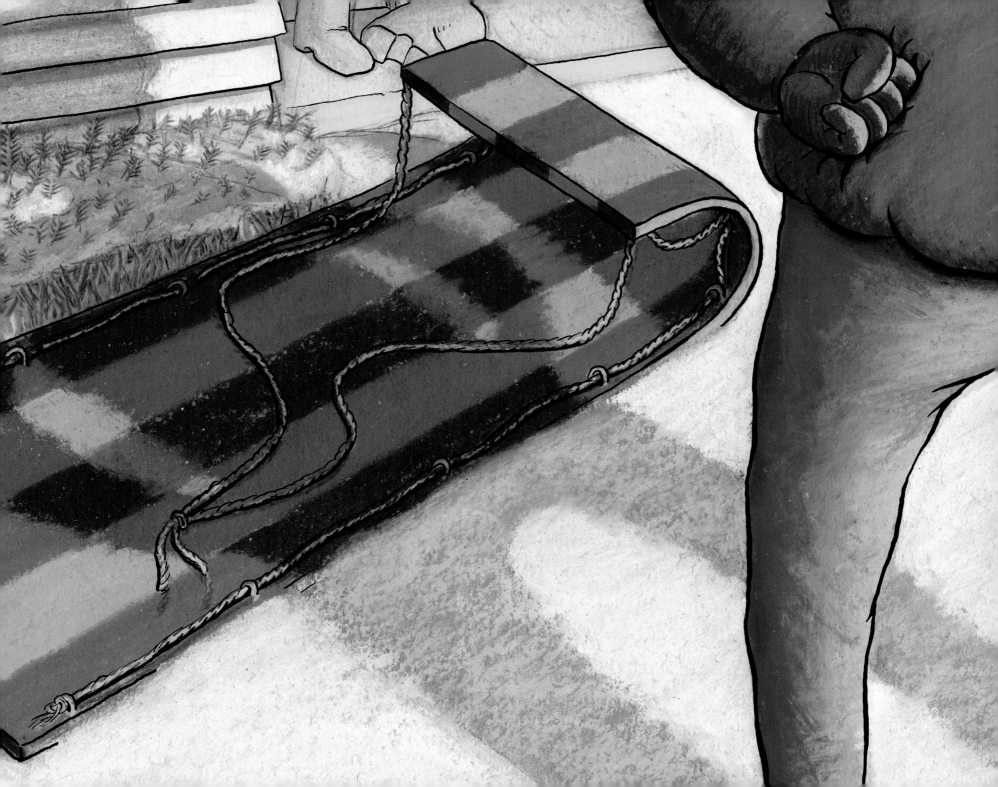

Quickly she tied old blankets and gunny sacks onto the toboggan with twine and dragged the toboggan to the far field by the woods.

Presto watched with hopeful eyes as Oma rubbed the all-white calf to warm it, and then lifted it onto the toboggan. She tied the calf to the toboggan so it wouldn't fall off, and then covered it with blankets.

The deep snow and heavy load on the toboggan tired Oma. It was a long and slow walk back. But she and Presto were happy to get to the barn with a final pull.

That day the children rushed home after school and begged to know if the newborn calf had been found.

Oma smiled. "Let's all go to the barn," she suggested.

Lying comfortably in warm and bright yellow straw was the all-white calf, with the almost-all-white cow standing nearby. The children listened silently with shining eyes as Oma explained how she found the calf and pulled it to the barn on the toboggan.

"Now I know that you children always think of wonderful names for the animals on our farm," continued Oma, "but this time I would like to name the all-white calf."

"Why, Mama?" asked the youngest child.

Oma paused, and then whispered, "Because today I found a miracle."

And the seven children cheered!

Oma had chosen the perfect name.

And Oma's grandchildren, who listened to the story on a snowy day, cheered too.

They thought the name "Miracle" was as perfect as eating Oma's freshly baked cookies with a glass of milk.